Uncle Victor

by Rosary Hartel O'Neill

A SAMUEL FRENCH ACTING EDITION

SAMUEL FRENCH

FOUNDED 1830

NEW YORK HOLLYWOOD LONDON TORONTO

SAMUELFRENCH.COM

ISBN 978-0-573-69761-6   Printed in U.S.A.   #23046

MUSIC USE NOTE

Licensees are solely responsible for obtaining formal written permission from copyright owners to use copyrighted music in the performance of this play and are strongly cautioned to do so. If no such permission is obtained by the licensee, then the licensee must use only original music that the licensee owns and controls. Licensees are solely responsible and liable for all music clearances and shall indemnify the copyright owners of the play and their licensing agent, Samuel French, Inc., against any costs, expenses, losses and liabilities arising from the use of music by licensees.

**IMPORTANT BILLING AND CREDIT
REQUIREMENTS**

All producers of *UNCLE VICTOR must* give credit to the Author of the Play in all programs distributed in connection with performances of the Play, and in all instances in which the title of the Play appears for the purposes of advertising, publicizing or otherwise exploiting the Play and/or a production. The name of the Author *must* appear on a separate line on which no other name appears, immediately following the title and *must* appear in size of type not less than fifty percent of the size of the title type.

CHARACTERS

RANDOLPH TROWELL (DOLPH) – a retired professor

ELLEN BARNES TROWELL – his wife, age twenty-seven

SOPHIE MALLORY TROWELL – his daughter by his first wife

LOUISE MALLORY (MAMERE) – mother of the professor's first wife

VICTOR – her son

DAVID AUGUST GREENAN – a doctor

MARIE GAUDET – an old nurse

UNCLE VICTOR was first performed in October 2000 at the Chamber Theatre, Budapest, Hungary.

Dedicated to the North American Program at Bonn University, where the play was written, and Lothar Honnighausen and Claus Daufenbach, who provided the fellowship, giving me time to write.

ACT ONE

Scene 1

(The gallery of Waverly, the Trowell family sugar cane plantation in South Louisiana, 1899. **AUGUST GREENAN***, a handsome, awkward young doctor, 29, sits sleeping in a chair. The old* **NURSE** *hums a spiritual "Rock of Ages," stands, removes the bottle from in front of the doctor, then exits.* **MAMERE***, an imperious but forgetful matron, enters with a candle.)*

*(**SOUND:** Wind)*

MAMERE. Where's Rosalie, Bertha, Ella?

DOCTOR. Careful with the candle.

MAMERE. I got to come from way in back of my house. *(Calls out)* James! Andrew! Clifford!

DOCTOR. They're gone, Mrs. Mallory

MAMERE. Nobody gets the door at my house. *(Paces)*

DOCTOR. For God's sake, sit.

MAMERE. Bertha! Verma! Rosalie!

DOCTOR. I'm Dr. Greenan. Augie Greenan.

MAMERE. I can't remember.

DOCTOR. You sent me to medical school—

MAMERE. Nobody sweeps the gallery?

DOCTOR. From spare change in your kitchen tin—

MAMERE. Dust all over the woodwork. Grass overgrown—

DOCTOR. Let me help you.

MAMERE. Statues crushed. There's the head of one over there.

DOCTOR. Sit, Mrs. Mallory.

MAMERE. The gates are shattered. A sundial disappeared overnight.

DOCTOR. Shouldn't you be asleep?

MAMERE. I can't rest when Waverly is falling apart. Shutters flap. I don't want to tell Mama because I'm not sure if she's alive or dead. *(Calls)* Mama.

DOCTOR. She's dead.

MAMERE. I didn't know. How long?

DOCTOR. Few years after— *(DOCTOR starts to drink)*

MAMERE. The war. I remember! But where's my daughter?

DOCTOR. Miss Rachelle? She passed.

MAMERE. Her too? You're lying.

DOCTOR. Why would I do that? I'm a doctor. I'm too tired.

MAMERE. Because you think I can't take it, but I'm strong as a warrior, you see. I'm a Mallory, and I'll stand tall by Waverly like the front gate. I was the first child after six boys. That's why as a girl they called me Loui, and when I didn't inherit the family carriage, I took a sledgehammer and broke all the windows. I was tough as the boys. My father was so hard, he was a pilot fish. He fed off my mother, leaving her at the mercy of her mental phantoms, which became real with my brothers' deaths during the war. All five. *(DOCTOR says "five" with her. He knows the story.)* Strength is an ordinary component of every woman. The sooner she breaks off the pattern of dependency on men, the better. But it's imbedded in our blood. We've been doing this since we were sitting round the fire, lounging in our big beds, excusing men who made us suffer and sewing our feelings into quilts.

(NURSE enters)

NURSE. I've such a backache. God. Five-thirty in the morning. *(Nods. To Mamere)* What you doing up?

MAMERE. Watching. There're prowlers like termites waiting to eat us. *(Laughs)* Good you don't have a wooden leg.

NURSE. I ain't got time for jokes. I'm tired. You know I can't sleep when I hear you poking about. Come on back to bed.

MAMERE. I'm not sleepy.

NURSE. Not after you got me up. *(Takes her arm)* Look at you. Clothes a mess. Hair in your face. That ain't no way to come outside. My back's so stiff.

MAMERE. Quiet. Or I'll call Mama.

(NURSE and MAMERE exit. Alone, the DOCTOR drinks. NURSE reenters, tries to get the drink from the DOCTOR.)

NURSE. Why you got to come here at dawn? Wake the old folks. It's a crying shame. You can't start doctoring with a drink in your hand. How old are you? Twenty something. When you start drinking at twenty, at thirty, you're gone.

DOCTOR. Life stinks.

NURSE. I know you want me to go on to bed; that's what you want. But you ain't going to get that. I knew your Mama and Papa before they died and I sure ain't going to let you sleep with no bottle. *(Picks up her quilt and sews)*

DOCTOR. I don't need anyone.

NURSE. I know something's eating you from the way you grumbling, looking at me from the side. I done seen that look before.

DOCTOR. I'm fine. *(Wipes his eyes)*

NURSE. Why you drinking? You don't like doctoring?

DOCTOR. In Louisiana people are idiots.

NURSE. Now you started doctoring, you don't like us. It's too late for that. They be people up and down the road is starving. Children who happy for a crust of bread. Old people so weak they can't get out the chair. You think 'cause you sad, and you drink, the world going to get better; well, you ain't the first one been hurting and you sure ain't going to be the last. You go to Church? You got that pagan smirk on your face. You done figured it all out.

DOCTOR. Look, I need some time—

NURSE. I ain't going to let you make love to no bottle when there's women all over South Louisiana wanting to be married to some fine young doctor. You lonely? What wrong with you, you don't see that? Me, I "jumped the broom" at fifteen. There are some things ain't right. Ain't right for you to be sitting here drinking. What kind of doctor you going to be with the shakes?

DOCTOR. I don't drink when I'm working.

NURSE. Not yet.

DOCTOR. I don't have the hardness for medicine. For this damn yellow fever. *(Speaks without emotion. He is tired and burned out)*

NURSE. Sit still, can't you—

DOCTOR. I like twitching. If I'm still, I suffocate. Then there're always these unexpected shocks. Yesterday it was this boy, a field hand. *(Pause)* I've got all my patients' names and addresses in this little book but I don't know which ones are dead or alive. I'm always thinking, I'm going to be there when a patient dies, but most times I am not. *(Laughs bitterly)* I've been in mourning for three hours. But that's behind me. I apologize. Thing is...I don't know why he died. I could dress up some stupid explanations. I can't understand—

NURSE. Perhaps you ain't supposed to. There are some things we can't do nothing about. Rest. *(Takes bottle and exits.)*

DOCTOR. I don't know where to go from here. I'll let you know when I've an idea.

(VICTOR MALLORY, 42, awakens from under a blanket on the wicker love seat.)

VICTOR. *(To the DOCTOR)* What're you doing here?

DOCTOR. Thrashing about with good intent. You thought I was your brother-in-law.

VICTOR. Sixty-five years of self-indulgence. He's a catastrophe about to happen.

DOCTOR. How are you managing? You tell me the truth; I'll tell you the truth.

VICTOR. I'm sick because he's back. I not only direct the peripheral characters; I think I am one. Wait till you see the wife he's got, and the man can barely walk. When she walks in, everyone pivots in her direction.

DOCTOR. Marrying outside one's age range is the ultimate transgression

VICTOR. Why did the professor get everything from life, even a beautiful wife, even the second time?

DOCTOR. You don't know he's happy.

VICTOR. Please. She never tells him what to do. She just suggests a thing from which the result would be fabulous.

DOCTOR. Women don't interest me.

VICTOR. Lucky you.

DOCTOR. You idolized him before.

VICTOR. People who're figureheads represent a particular type of duplicity.

DOCTOR. Someone said he was the most famous professor at Tulane.

VICTOR. He's a cold, calculating fiend who's capable of kindness but it's a rarity.

*(***SOPHIE***, 27, the professor's daughter by his first wife, enters.)*

SOPHIE. Good morning, Doctor. I see you've already arrived.

DOCTOR. Good morning.

VICTOR. Sophie used to help me. Now, she follows her father around. We're in competition for worst place. We've to scramble for the crumbs.

SOPHIE. I'm helping Papa with an article for "Harper's."

VICTOR. Stuck on this father who drives her back and forth and screams for me.

DOCTOR. Famous men get lots of attention. *(To* **SOPHIE***)* I'd like to stay the night, if you don't mind.

SOPHIE. Wonderful. It's always a splendid treat when you do.

VICTOR. *(Stamps ground)* The ground has a wetness to it. You feel it? You can't bribe the help to deepen the drainage outlets.

*(*RANDOLPH *TROWELL, 65, in ill health, enters.)*

RANDOLPH. Don't let me stop your stimulating conversation about carefully drained lawns.

*(*ELLEN*, 28, gorgeous, enters in a décolleté black silk gown. She looks at the* **DOCTOR***, and he looks back. She pulls her robe around her.)*

ELLEN. I didn't know anyone was here.

DOCTOR. Apologies.

RANDOLPH. This is Dr. Greenan. My in-laws financed him through school. Here's Ellen. The replacement wife. *(*ELLEN *exits.)*

VICTOR. We'll take that in the jocular vein which it invites.

DOCTOR. How are you feeling?

RANDOLPH. Great till I saw you.

VICTOR. *(To* **DOCTOR***)* Part of his charm is his shamelessness. We'll ignore that.

RANDOLPH. Let's give thanks for something. It's not a bad day. It's a bad decade.

DOCTOR. Have you been feeling poorly?

RANDOLPH. *(Sits)* All I wanted was to sit a few days in a row, so God took standing from me. Do you know what that's like, always gauging whether you can make it someplace?

VICTOR. I never go anywhere.

RANDOLPH. Your personality reflects it. Victor's not too bright, but he can count from one to nine.

VICTOR. *(To* **DOCTOR***)* He makes me feel like I'm about an inch lower than my left ear.

SOPHIE. Papa. Would you like some milk?

RANDOLPH. Coffee in my room. And cake. *(As* **SOPHIE** *helps him out.)* Preferably Bavarian Cream. I've an appointment with death, but first I've an appointment with life.

*(*RANDOLPH *and* SOPHIE *exit.)*

VICTOR. He swoops in like a mynah bird with mange. Lands and the room goes dark. Still he's got this wife. She was lovely yesterday, but she's even lovelier today. And the man's one of the great bores of the nineteenth century! *(Looks in* **ELLEN**'s *direction)* What do you think about her? Nice to be young.

DOCTOR. I can't remember.

VICTOR. She's a romantic. To be that, she has to adopt a disguise. Needs twenty-four hours to wash her hair. She drifts about while I'm going into a serious decline.

DOCTOR. She's obviously not faithful.

VICTOR. Course she is. She's Catholic. And he had her first. There's no sin anymore, no salvation anymore, and I don't think there's going to be any sex anymore. I'm a little strapped by life right now. His arrival was a great interruption. He doesn't belong here. The person who did died. He eats nonstop. Sleeps half the day.

DOCTOR. He's sensible.

VICTOR. Conniving. All the help know he came from nothing. He's screwed up the schedule, and this estate, which barely paid for itself, is in debt. The help used to come in at eight, now he eats at five in the morning, eleven at night. Servants lining up to watch. There's no cohesive force here. I move about like a guest whose host has left. He laughs when I say we are going bankrupt. My teeth chatter at night. I can't control them. Our expenses have tripled, and sugar prices have dropped.

DOCTOR. When's he going back to New Orleans?

VICTOR. Never. He's retired. He'll stay here forever, grumbling till he rots in place and I become chauffeur of the dead. I don't know why I didn't see through him. I guess I was too busy being young. Sister and I did everything we could to protect Waverly, but he finagled and got it for himself. *(Pause)* Mamere used to say, "Don't work for the second wife." How true! The first wife penny-pinches, only for the second wife to appear in furs and diamonds and loll about.

DOCTOR. You don't like your step sister-in-law?

VICTOR. She's the laziest, most exquisite thing I've ever seen. You think she'll leave Randolph?

(ELLEN walks in quickly. She gets some paper.)

ELLEN. Excuse me.

VICTOR. *(To ELLEN)* Ah, Sleeping Beauty. They say when Sleeping Beauty wakes up she's fifty years old.

ELLEN. Pardon me. I've the hardest time finding things. I'm between a this and a that.

VICTOR. Join us.

ELLEN. *(Glancing at the DOCTOR)* It's Sunday morning, and much too early to speak.

(ELLEN exits.)

VICTOR. Did you get a look? That dress could get me in a lot of trouble.

DOCTOR. She seems extraordinary to me.

VICTOR. Then she is, isn't she?

DOCTOR. But overdone.

VICTOR. I wouldn't mind a bit of overdone woman. I'm forty-two but I look fifty. What do you prescribe?

DOCTOR. Sit. Take a deep breath. And count to three.

VICTOR. What? One, two, three.

DOCTOR. Now, sit and read the Bible.

VICTOR. The Bible?

DOCTOR. "Thou shalt not covet thy neighbor's wife." I'm going for a walk.

(ELLEN enters.)

ELLEN. Victor, Randolph has instructions for you.

VICTOR. But is he nice? Used to be old people were the kind ones because they took time to think; now kindness isn't popular.

(VICTOR exits.)

DOCTOR. Sophie wrote your husband's not well.

ELLEN. Today he's improved.

DOCTOR. *(Awkward pause. Eyeing her dress)* Fetching dress.

ELLEN. My Natasha gown? I usually wear dark colors, so when I wear fuchsia I feel naughty. Why are you staring?

DOCTOR. I'm used to examining people.

(SOPHIE enters with coffee.)

SOPHIE. I'll set the table.

ELLEN. *(To SOPHIE)* Call the maid.

SOPHIE. We let so many servants go.

ELLEN. So ends another grand tradition of grace!

DOCTOR. I'll freshen up.

(DOCTOR and SOPHIE exit as VICTOR reenters.)

VICTOR. There's letters and packages for you and Randolph blocking my office. A trunk of—

ELLEN. My new hat.

VICTOR. From the most expensive modiste in New Orleans.

ELLEN. A little color in a gray life.

VICTOR. Is all this necessary?

ELLEN. Fabrics don't last long in this climate.

VICTOR. Style is costly. That's why I look like I do.

ELLEN. My husband'll reimburse you.

VICTOR. With what? *(Hands* **ELLEN** *some invoices)* This was bought on credit. You can't live in the grand manner if we don't produce sufficient cane.

ELLEN. Who's living in the grand manner?

VICTOR. This house is the size of three city mansions. When I suggest economizing, your husband looks off at the oak trees.

*(***MAMERE*** and* **NURSE** *enter.)*

MAMERE. I got a letter from the Women's Guild.

NURSE. Your mother is her old self. It's a miracle how her fog has lifted.

MAMERE. They're creating an archive of the professor's unpublished articles.

NURSE. *(To* **VICTOR***, whispers)* Maybe she should rise each morning at five.

MAMERE. We could use your help, Victor, with the cataloguing, especially the Tulane lectures.

NURSE. Your mother spoke French today. She was so sharp.

MAMERE. Nurse asked me all the phrases I knew. My family spoke French in the 1700's. *"On parle francais depuis des centaines d'annees."* I'd like to talk to my son in French, but for him, The Misanthrope isn't even a title. I suppose it's too late. Victor's forty-two but he looks almost as old as I do. When Victor was little, all he wanted to be was smart, you remember? Go like the professor on a ride of wealth and fame. I felt as confused then as I do now about where he's going. The boy doesn't think. If Victor wanted to fly, he'd paste feathers on his arms and jump off a bridge. Even as a child he was maudlin. Liked big black hats and capes. You couldn't call him inside; if he wasn't completely wrecked, scratched, blood somewhere, torn clothes, he didn't feel like he'd played long enough. I don't know what charm is, but I know Victor doesn't have it.

NURSE. Let's go read in the garden.

MAMERE. The professor's always buying, while Victor's always selling. Why can't Victor imitate him? *(***MAMERE** *exits with the* **NURSE.** *The following lines overlap.)*

VICTOR. No one appreciates me or Waverly—

ELLEN. Who needs such a big house—

VICTOR. I'm orphaned in a way—

ELLEN. We spend our time on the gallery—

VICTOR. I've had to put up my life as collateral. Perhaps I should have left.

ELLEN. You could pack a suitcase and go now.

VICTOR. If only I had the energy.

ELLEN. Well, lie in the shade, wiggle your toes, and watch the sparrows till you get your personality back.

VICTOR. I don't want to be a drone.

ELLEN. Not too close.

VICTOR. I don't think one relationship should prevent another from flourishing. *(Walks over and puts his arm around her.)* You don't love Randolph. You don't hold hands in the dark anymore. That's the first step. Women who stay with men they don't love slowly deteriorate. One day you'll look in the mirror and think, whose worn face is that? You'll be old and you won't have tasted one of the great pleasures of life, sweetheart.

ELLEN. Don't touch me.

VICTOR. Three milligrams of Randolph will kill you. Walking him in, walking him out.

ELLEN. I'm no heroine. When I'm tired, I nap. *(Closes her eyes and tries to sleep.)*

VICTOR. Does he even talk to you?

ELLEN. I can live with him as long as—

VICTOR. You treat him like a spoiled boy, don't hold him accountable. Perhaps you won't outlive him. *(Grabs her face)* Look how your eyes have shrunk, your lips tightened, in the short time you've been here. He'll kill you just like he did my sister.

ELLEN. She died of a miscarriage.

VICTOR. Technically, but really from a broken heart. The professor ran to the city to forge a career.

ELLEN. I'm not like your sister. Let me rest. If by some merciful reason I fall asleep, I'll kill the man who wakes me up.

(DOCTOR reenters, followed by SOPHIE.)

DOCTOR. *(To ELLEN)* Look at that beautiful sky. Violet blue. Must be heaven, being embraced by that blue.

VICTOR. *(Looks at a letter. To the DOCTOR)* I forgot. A note for you. One of the field hands brought it. *(Sits with his ledger.)* The trouble with account books is they don't beckon. There's nothing interesting about finding someone who will loan you money again and again and still talk to you.

SOPHIE. Eat with us?

DOCTOR. *(Looks off)* I can't stay.

(SOPHIE exits. ELLEN has closed her eyes and drifted off.)

DOCTOR. *(Crosses and watches her)* You asleep? Where do you go when you're not here?

ELLEN. Nowhere.

DOCTOR. There are so many ways stillness treats our needs. Look, the sun's rising through the trees. In a half hour it's changed dramatically. Nothing is more uplifting than light through oak leaves. *(She opens her eyes.)* See them, allowing the sun to come in, turning up to receive it. They've a heliotropic life *(Takes out his pocket watch.)* I wish we measured time by the sun and not by the clock, like we used to.

ELLEN. Me too.

DOCTOR. We know the sun's not going to be there forever. We appreciate the enchantment of the moment.

ELLEN. How far away do you live?

DOCTOR. Twenty miles up river.

ELLEN. Do you ride without a stop?

DOCTOR. If I'm tired, looking for emptiness, for some way to clear the slate in my life, I stop my horse and watch the Mississippi. The movement of the water, its changing currents give the soul its contemplation. *(Gazes at* **ELLEN**) There's something mysterious and female about water, and that river has a primal connection to it. Her power comes from the sky and goes through the earth to the psyche of the underworld. She's deep, primordial and lovely with an extraordinary sheen. If you meditate, put your soul into her all the way, you can see her, feel her, lose yourself in her violence. There are so many ways her fullness heals me. *(Pause)* Would you like a drink? With more drinks, you see more.

ELLEN. Too early.

DOCTOR. Never too early. It's always too late. One refusal doesn't mean a final refusal.

ELLEN. How do you have time to watch the water?

VICTOR. *(Watches the* **DOCTOR** *and* **ELLEN***)* I could use a drink.

DOCTOR. I study whatever I can't get out of my mind. Most times it's the Mississippi. Until I was fifteen, I went to sleep with the Great River in my head, dreaming of lost treasure. Summers I used to work on the salvage boats that raised ships from the bottom. That river contains water our Indian ancestors rode on. It's in our bones. *(Looks up, breathes deep)* Sometimes when I look at that river, she scares me. The Mississippi is violent, and high water magnifies her violence. She's complicated, folded together, irrational, and she rises every night to meet these torrential rains. *(Chuckles)* On the river, rain is never received with great joy; it's received with mourning. A river should be predictable. The last thing you want is a wild force. The Greeks imagined Neptune with a pitchfork and snakes for hair. You can't control him easily. Once I saw a whole tree sucked under by the current. Last week I watched a house sink in a storm. The land caved away, a hundred yards at a time. The tide washed against the front steps and boom. It was gone.

ELLEN. Why don't people do something?

DOCTOR. The Feds haven't fixed the levees since the war. Locals argue...refusing to build outlets while the water rises higher. How can a hill contain all that? When a levee five stories high cracks, the water will explode like a tidal wave.

(Sound: Carriage)

SOPHIE. Your carriage is here.

DOCTOR. Thanks.

VICTOR. A doctor who's concerned with nature. I suppose you devote Sunday to the orphans.

DOCTOR. Somebody should.

SOPHIE. *(To* **DOCTOR***)* When are you coming back?

DOCTOR. Don't know. House calls are risky. You're not in control of time. Look at those white azaleas. My carriage seems as though it's surrounded by clouds.

ELLEN. See you soon.

DOCTOR. I hope. When I come here, I find such peace.

VICTOR. You have to come here to feel?

*(***DOCTOR** *and* **SOPHIE** *exit.)*

ELLEN. *(To* **VICTOR***)* Why needle the doctor? You dislike free spirits?

VICTOR. Doctors are always right, which is one of the annoying things about them.

ELLEN. How long have you known the doctor?

VICTOR. Since childhood. I never noticed. *(Pause)* I don't want to be one of those men who learn about love as he's relinquishing it. I watch you, and I'm...renewed; I ask myself...could you get a divorce...

ELLEN. And the professor?

VICTOR. You are not intimate with him?

ELLEN. *(Laughs)* In the South we go to great trouble not to get to the point. I admire my husband. He—

VICTOR. Bought you.

ELLEN. I adore gifted people. Could you take me to Paris?

VICTOR. Paris, Rome, London.

ELLEN. Who'd look after Waverly and hold up the family?

VICTOR. We family members steal from each other all the time. It's part of the tradition. *(He kisses her violently.)*

ELLEN. The last thing I want is a raving lunatic.

(SOUND: Wind.)

(LIGHTS: Lights out.)

*(***ELLEN*** costume change. **VICTOR** sits. When we hear crickets, bring up the lights.)*

Scene 2

(The estate. Night. The **PROFESSOR** *sleeps, snoring.* **ELLEN** *sits watching him with uncovered disgust. He wakes up, and she is disciplined again.)*

RANDOLPH. What's that?

ELLEN. It's me.

RANDOLPH. I'd an awful dream. I was in this swamp. The water was rising and I was sinking, waterlogged from the feet to the head, the skin floating off my body. I was moving toward my own death. Oh God. I don't know whether I drowned or not but I woke up with this headache.

ELLEN. You want...some Beaujolais?

RANDOLPH. Victor hardly knows a good wine. He's ignorant of civilized tastes.

ELLEN. Perhaps the doctor could prescribe—

RANDOLPH. I'd brilliant colleagues. Students waited in the hallway to hear me.

ELLEN. I remember.

RANDOLPH. Do you? There are a lot of dead people in my memory. I don't use it anymore. Where did all that genius go? *(Pause)* And why do you look at me with those dead eyes?

ELLEN. I'm not blaming you. It's not your fault—

RANDOLPH. There's death in life, too. Death to things that are young. Come here. It's only at the end of the day I start to feel my age. I feel fine till nine at night.

ELLEN. I'm getting older by the minute.

RANDOLPH. No, you're not.

ELLEN. I looked in the mirror and saw a wrinkle radiating from the corner of my eye.

RANDOLPH. Come, sugar. Don't upset yourself.

ELLEN. I don't want to get old, be ugly.

RANDOLPH. You won't. Time is on the side of things young. Let's get in bed, go to places where only you and I can fit.

ELLEN. You go on.

RANDOLPH. I can't sleep alone. I've to feel you by me to breathe. If only I didn't have this nagging pain...It's like being in jail . . .longing for what went before and fearing what will come.

ELLEN. I'm...sorry but I'm indisposed.

RANDOLPH. Don't cry wolf with me.

ELLEN. Maybe by the end of the week, I'll be up to—

RANDOLPH. You think I don't know I make you sick? Go sleep in the guest room. Let everyone know we aren't having relations. Parade through the house with your pillow. You've that shiny new ring, and you're an angry woman.

ELLEN. I...I...care for you.

RANDOLPH. You used me...you wanted money and prestige—

ELLEN. Who doesn't like comfort?

RANDOLPH. I don't mind if you want more rings, a new gown. I miss the lazy evening soirees, and even the drizzle that set them off. Embrace me.

ELLEN. Not in here.

RANDOLPH. Where then?

ELLEN. I'm not against affection—

RANDOLPH. Ah-ha. You want me to catch you. Play cat and mouse.

ELLEN. I'll join you.

RANDOLPH. I got you! Ah-ha. Put your hand here.

ELLEN. Oh, God, don't start!

RANDOLPH. Touch me.

ELLEN. Don't.

RANDOLPH. More.

ELLEN. Oh, God. Oh, my.

(He forces her to kiss him in an attempt to make love.)

RANDOLPH. I'm taking what's mine.

ELLEN. Oh, no! Don't!

(MAMERE stands at the door with a gun.)

MAMERE. Stop! Or I'll kill you.

RANDOLPH. No! It's me...Randolph . . .

ELLEN. Put down the gun.

MAMERE. Who are you?

RANDOLPH. One of her foggy days.

ELLEN. His wife.

MAMERE. Impossible.

RANDOLPH. *(Screams)* Victor, come get your mother.

(RANDOLPH exits.)

ELLEN. What's wrong?

MAMERE. Everything's dusty in Rachelle's room. I don't know where she is.

RANDOLPH. Victor!

MAMERE. The goal of motherhood is the crafting of children. Rachelle was my crown jewel.

ELLEN. Sit. Tell me about her.

MAMERE. She was jovial—gathering people together artfully with some attention to detail. I can see her imagination breathing in things, even though she's disappeared.

ELLEN. That's nice.

MAMERE. You remind me of her, strangely. Beauty was what she was interested in, fixing herself up and making herself look pretty. *(VICTOR enters.)* She loved life. There was always a stimulating conversation going on between her and me.

RANDOLPH. *(O.S.)* Victor, where are you?

MAMERE. Victor? What do you want him for? Rachelle was happy at the core of her being, while Victor wears a permanent scowl. He's my nemesis. You can't separate him from his angry ghosts.

ELLEN. That's too bad.

MAMERE. It is, because when you're around him, you've heard every complaint possible. Five o'clock sherry with Victor is the closest thing to hell. I try to have a conversation but there's nothing there. If you connect the dots in the lines of his life, you'd draw an empty well. The only difference between Victor now and as a child is he wears suits, not knickers. Men grow up when they want to or they don't grow up at all. He's forty-two and still toddling about.

(VICTOR *enters with* **RANDOLPH***, walks over to* **MAMERE***. She lifts the gun.)*

VICTOR. It's Victor. Give me the gun.

MAMERE. Who?

VICTOR. Your son...the toddler, although most times I feel like the family slave. *(Takes the gun)* The gun, Mama.
*(*NURSE *arrives. Hurries to* **MAMERE***.)*

NURSE. She stole the gun out the cabinet. I can't leave her for a minute. She likes to scare people, but she's harmless.

VICTOR. I'll put her to bed.

MAMERE. No, I'm waiting for Rachelle.

VICTOR. You know she's passed.

NURSE. *(To* **VICTOR***)* Don't you be taking my job. *(To* **MAMERE***)* Come on now.

VICTOR. *(To* **NURSE***)* She's got to accept Rachelle's dead.

NURSE. Let her live with her own truth.

MAMERE. What'd Victor say?

NURSE. Nothing. Most men make you feel bad about things. I don't listen to them.

RANDOLPH. Will you all get out!

NURSE. *(To* **RANDOLPH***)* Why don't you go to sleep with your wife?

RANDOLPH. I intend to.

VICTOR. I don't have a family about me. I've some estranged people who're driving me out of my mind—

NURSE. How can I bed her for the night if you don't keep quiet? Old people are like children. They want attention and closeness.

VICTOR. I'll walk her.

NURSE. No, you just play take-away. She so bored she don't know what to do with herself. You say I love you, but I can't pay for anything. She don't go nowhere. Buy nothing. Invite anybody to the house. I love you, you say, but you don't take no time for her. She want to go places, do things. You so busy running Waverly, you don't see. And you a Louisiana white man, so you don't have to.

*(*VICTOR, **NURSE**, **MAMERE** *exit. Enter* **SOPHIE** *with a candle and soup.)*

SOPHIE. Papa, you're feeling better? The doctor arrived.

RANDOLPH. Suppose he's here to steal our liquor. Go...comb your hair. I should work on you. A successful teacher doesn't change the mind, but the personality of the student.

SOPHIE. *(To* **ELLEN***)* You look exhausted.

ELLEN. I am.

(ELLEN slips out)

SOPHIE. This chicken soup should restore your health. It's marvelous to think Cook makes great soup. It contains a strained broth and chicken.

RANDOLPH. Where did Ellen go?

SOPHIE. You're perspiring.

RANDOLPH. I want turtle soup...finished with sherry. Tell Cook to take one shelled, skinned, and cleaned turtle. About two pounds of flesh.

SOPHIE. Don't spill that.

RANDOLPH. It's tepid.

SOPHIE. If it's too hot, it'll burn your throat.

RANDOLPH. Reheat it.

SOPHIE. Heavens. Eat a few sips.

RANDOLPH. Too cold.

SOPHIE. Eat please. I can't keep running back and forth.

RANDOLPH. Well, don't.

SOPHIE. *(Swallows hard)* Papa, I need you to...improve...so you can help Uncle. Sugar is a difficult, year-round operation.

RANDOLPH. As your mother has passed, I take the liberty of telling you, you move like a field hand.

SOPHIE. I'll...work on it, Papa. You've never told us about your debts. *(SOPHIE takes out some papers.)* Money's due on these purchases.

RANDOLPH. Is it? Ha!

SOPHIE. Is Uncle authorized...to pay these bills? We've budgeted every penny. This month's income must go to insurance and taxes—so officials don't seize the house. So many repairs have to be done.

RANDOLPH. It's not expensive to make repairs. But you have to work along with people. And that Victor's not used to!

SOPHIE. If only it were that simple. Chairs need reupholstering. Doorknobs replating. The entire house needs painting . . .

RANDOLPH. Do it.

SOPHIE. How? A codicil...to the will gives Waverly to you till I marry and you're spending money on the wrong things. Soon all we'll have is soul and the clothes on our backs.

RANDOLPH. Are you trying to make me feel guilty I just gave the Church a statue...in honor of your mother, and the deceased members of the family?

SOPHIE. But how can you spend money, when...half of the help have asked for raises? The house is falling apart. Two bad crops or a serious flood and we'll lose Waverly. Now we've paid off the heavy mortgages, we need you to cut back...Uncle's working under wretched conditions.

RANDOLPH. Is that why he naps midday?

SOPHIE. We split the responsibilities. I care for the—

RANDOLPH. Here's how I see it. Victor's well has run dry, and his future's behind him. He's not broke, you see. He's having a hard time meeting the standards he's developed. I don't owe him a nickel. *(Dumps the soup.)* Get my wife.

SOPHIE. Get her yourself.

RANDOLPH. Get her myself?

SOPHIE. You want to squeeze this place dry, but there's no money left. I won't let you lay Uncle in a box like you did Mama.

RANDOLPH. I just bought a statue.

SOPHIE. Out of guilt! That's right! She wanted to keep you so bad she worried herself to an early grave. On your last visit, she made me do her up, powder, rouge, and all. She knew without beauty she wouldn't see you.

RANDOLPH. Liar. I came home the minute I heard—

SOPHIE. She was dying. Where did they find you? In some woman's apartment, Uncle said.

RANDOLPH. I see. Victor's turned you against me.

SOPHIE. Not true.

RANDOLPH. What did he or Rachelle ever do?

SOPHIE. Plenty.

RANDOLPH. Rachelle preferred Waverly to me, and Waverly fed her fears.

SOPHIE. Mama was valiant.

RANDOLPH. In death maybe but not in life. She was nervous near a horse. Scared of steamboats. Petrified of trains. I'd time to write because I married Madame Panic. I begged her to visit. She'd agree then change her mind or catch a cold. She was selfish. God rest her soul.

SOPHIE. How can you say that! About Mama!

RANDOLPH. She didn't care about me.

SOPHIE. She was so sweet.

RANDOLPH. To you maybe. She taught you to resent your father and she made sure I was a man you barely knew.

(Enter **VICTOR***)*

VICTOR. I thought I'd barge in New Orleans style. Storm's building out front. *(To* **SOPHIE***)* I'll sit with him.

SOPHIE. You've got to...get up early.

*(***SOPHIE** *leaves.)*

RANDOLPH. You gave the order—

VICTOR. Yes. The cutting, loading and hauling start tomorrow. Cutting should be easier this year. I've restricted the acres devoted to cane.

(The following speeches overlap.)

RANDOLPH. Who authorized that?

VICTOR. Do I need authorization?

RANDOLPH. Decisions shouldn't be made precipitously—

VICTOR. I'm not your student—

RANDOLPH. All men must learn to think smart—

VICTOR. I don't have to listen to this.

RANDOLPH. You've made stupid, stupid decisions.

VICTOR. Men say, "I don't have to take this" when they should leave.

(NURSE enters.)

(VICTOR exits.)

RANDOLPH. Why am I so tired?

NURSE. You're sixty-five.

RANDOLPH. Do you know what it feels like to be surrounded by idiots, to be happily married, and not to be able to rest?

NURSE. You got problems.

RANDOLPH. I've a wonderful young wife who's driving me out of my mind. Waking up between hot sheets, a candle glaring in the window.

SOUND: Fade up slowly WIND.)

NURSE. I couldn't sleep after the war. I'd walk around Waverly and think I saw soldiers. Three Yankee soldiers approached me but I scared them off with a gun. *(To* **RANDOLPH***)* Storm's picking up. Let me take you to bed. I'll sing you a song my Mama sang to me. "Lord guide my feet on wandering paths."

(RANDOLPH and NURSE exit. VICTOR and ELLEN enter. She does not see RANDOLPH.)

ELLEN. Randolph? *(To* **VICTOR***)* Good, he's gone. I'm worn out with him. The main cause for women's death is childbirth, cuts, then tedious husbands.

VICTOR. I love the way you talk, move. I don't care what you say.

ELLEN. *(Focuses on her drink)* Don't distract me.

VICTOR. *(Hurt)* I was trying to compliment you. *(Looks out)* Rains could flood the fields. Cane could all be drowned out. Does the professor worry?

ELLEN. Why do you do it?

VICTOR. Revenge is a good motive. It's acceptable in Southern circles. *(Takes a drink)*

ELLEN. Why don't you leave for the city, make something of yourself?

VICTOR. Whenever I get in the carriage to go there, my hands shake. I've to turn around and come back.

ELLEN. Once the professor improves, we'll go to Paris, I'll drink champagne in a café by Saint Paul's.

VICTOR. Notre Dame.

ELLEN. Watch boats glide down the Rhine?

VICTOR. Seine.

ELLEN. Drink Chateaubriand that tastes like rose petals and have Cotes du Rhone you can cut with a fork.

SOUND: "Let Me Call You Sweetheart."

ELLEN. The night Watchman. I'd better go.

VICTOR. *(Calls out)* Play.

(Night watchman plays "Let Me Call You Sweetheart." **VICTOR** *hands her a box.)*

A few elegant pleasures left. One is a wrapped gift.

ELLEN. Oh, my! Jeweled hairpins?

VICTOR. Great Aunt Jane's. Here, we do have heirlooms. Hold one to the moon.

ELLEN. It does glitter. But I don't go anywhere. I can't accept these...I'd best be leaving. Now in Paris, I'd take your jewelry. I'd camouflage these shiny pins among my satins, ribbons, and pearls. But where would I wear them here?

(ELLEN exits. Alone, **VICTOR** *drinks excessively.)*

SOUND: Waltz.

VICTOR. Ten years ago I saw her at a ball in New Orleans—glowing like a star in a velvet sky. Two lazy-eyed Louisiana boys stood by her, both thinking they were her escort. She was just there. Everyone else eclipsed. An invasion of beauty. If only I'd pursued her. She'd be lying next to me. *(Sound out.)* Thigh to thigh. Instead I financed his lectures, tours, articles so he could arrive with the masterpiece in hand. Why? Why?

SOUND: Scene change music.

ACT 2

Scene 1

(SOUND: "Oh Suzanna.")

(Several hours later, **VICTOR** *is passed out on the love seat.* **DOCTOR** *enters.)*

DOCTOR. Play some more. *("Oh Suzanna" is heard on a harmonica.)* Your mantle clock reads, "Hours do not count unless they are happy." Well, I found the moon tonight. I celebrated my birthday watching the moon. Expressing my thanks to all those brave doctors from my past. I'm the first doctor in my family. And the last. *(Looks about)* Where's the corpse?

VICTOR. Don't mock Randolph...so loudly.

DOCTOR. You can talk frankly, but I can't. He wears a flowered waistcoat and pointed boots, while you won't buy yourself a watch. And your sister-in-law's so unlike the rest of you. Gorgeous but scattered.

VICTOR. Sometimes she reads Virgil to the professor.

DOCTOR. Ah, let's have a brandy—Dance and sing loud. *(Sings with watchman playing)* "Oh Suzanna, oh don't you cry for me. For I come from Alabama with my banjo on my knee. It rained all night, the day I left. The weather it was dry . . ."

VICTOR. You're going to wake the professor.

DOCTOR. Let's wake the whole house and bring her out.

VICTOR. What a grand infantile comment.

DOCTOR. The things she can do with a ribbon or lace. She floats in with lavender preceding her. Brings in another century. I slept soundly till she crossed my path. Then, I lost the night. I would pay her to leave my thoughts. Now I'll go find her.

*(***DOCTOR** *exits and* **SOPHIE** *comes in.* **VICTOR** *drinks.)*

VICTOR. "Oh Suzanna oh don't you cry for me, for I . . ."

SOPHIE. Give men two drinks and they all talk alike: loud, loud, loud.

SOUND: Out

VICTOR. The doctor needed company.

SOPHIE. Let him pamper himself. If the doctor wants to drink all night, fine. But you can't. Tomorrow you'll feed stalks to the grinders. You need to be alert. If you must indulge, have one of Papa's Cuban cigars.

VICTOR. A man of discrimination doesn't steal. *(Stumbles.)* I'm fine.

(VICTOR exits on his knees.)

DOCTOR. Victor? Victor?

SOPHIE. He's gone to bed. Tomorrow he supervises men with knives.

DOCTOR. Cutting cane? I should respect that. *(Goes to get his coat, bumps into a table)* I feel so alert as the day commences. And foggy as it ends. I'm sorry. I better leave.

SOPHIE. You're tired. Sit a spell.

DOCTOR. I've so many patients. I can't just give them a remedy. I have to treat their gloom. Yellow fever everywhere, and no one knows the cause.

SOPHIE. Your voice is so soothing. You could improve anyone you talked to.

DOCTOR. You've hands like your mother. Long thin fingers. Oblong-shaped nails.

SOPHIE. You remember her?

DOCTOR. Vividly. Little boys love beauties. *(Pause)* You've grown into a woman and I hardly noticed. I'm sorry. I better leave.

SOPHIE. Won't you have a snack first? I enjoy eating at night. Should we have cheese or fruit?

DOCTOR. *(Continues drinking)* Both.

SOPHIE. Papa's a complete snob about what he keeps. The grapes are the size of plums. We've four or five proper wines.

DOCTOR. I think I can do two things at once: cure and live, and mostly I end up doing the curing thing. And doing it poorly. Have you been out there? The fields are under-staffed. Children and old people work till they drop. You can't be an effective doctor working in miserable conditions. Where's the unlimited power of science? I believe in progress, but we've to face it. People destroy each other, and they don't build a better life. They're all alone.

SOPHIE. And your family?

DOCTOR. Mine? All dead. I barely remember my sister and parents and don't want to. No. I live for my patients. They become family. "Can you cure me?" they ask. My job's to say yes, but how. Most times, I sleep with the question. For yellow fever, all we know is the reality we've been brought up in. But that reality isn't big enough to save them. Some die horribly. They say human means "of the earth," out of which comes humiliation...The fortunate fade into a quiet frenzy.

SOPHIE. How do you deal with it?

DOCTOR. Death? Not well. I go off alone and sit by the river, immobilized.

SOPHIE. And what do you do there?

DOCTOR. I play this game I've concocted where I imagine all unborn infants as little drops. That some of us have to pass on for others to enter the cycle. Still, each time I shut a patient's eyes, a part of me closes. I'm an old man for a young doctor; maybe I'd die soon.

SOPHIE. You're not yet thirty.

DOCTOR. I've a rundown body, old like a used book. *(Guzzles liquor)*

SOPHIE. You're a spirit-filled person and you've—

DOCTOR. If only I could go back to being a boy and relive what excited me.

SOPHIE. If I had a friend who admired you, could you...have...any feelings for her?

DOCTOR. I doubt it. For a long time, I haven't loved anyone—

SOPHIE. You never want to...settle down?

DOCTOR. I couldn't be a husband or father. Women want successful husbands, but they don't want to pay the price. The price of success is time. What's that slogan? "Work, work, work, and when you're tired, work some more." Spouses will hate you for that. They'll turn green when you leave the house. *(Rises)* And I'm always leaving, aren't I?

(DOCTOR exits. Moments later, ELLEN enters.)

ELLEN. Storm's lessening. What delicious air. Smells like magnolias and brandy. Where's the doctor?

SOPHIE. Gone.

ELLEN. Already? Our destinies have been parted by a few indirect steps. *(SOPHIE starts to exit.)* Sophie, no, wait. I want to apologize for how cold I've been. Well. You've been so sweet, and I'm a witch. It's strange having a stepdaughter—

SOPHIE. Who's older than you? I know.

(They both smile.)

ELLEN. I want us to be close. I miss having girls my age I can talk to.

SOPHIE. Oh, it's so good to hear you say that!

ELLEN. Let's drink to friendship.

SOPHIE. I've this secret I'm dying to tell someone.

ELLEN. About the doctor?

SOPHIE. You guessed. I can't believe what I just did. I made a proposal.

ELLEN. Wha'd you say?

SOPHIE. I asked him if he wanted to settle down...But he didn't realize the someone was me. *(Passes the mirror)* How terrible I'm not beautiful. In church I heard someone say, "She's such a sweet girl. But no beauty like her mother. She ought to buy dresses that make her look younger. She seems so matronly." Matronly!

ELLEN. You've nice hair—

SOPHIE. People always say that—When there's nothing else. Mamere says, "Men can talk about the women who raise the best children, keep the best house, bake

36

the best pies, but it's the beautiful women they come home to." *(Hands her a miniature)* Can you fix my hair like this miniature?

ELLEN. I don't want to look at pictures of other people's dead relatives.

SOPHIE. It went to a great exhibition. It was called "A Young Girl."

ELLEN. Who is she?

SOPHIE. Mama. Just lace my hair with silk ribbons.

ELLEN. Like in the picture. I can do that.

SOPHIE. Each night, I pray I'll wake up looking more like Mama, that one day I'll have tons of children and idle moments to play Mozart and remember her. *(NURSE has entered.)* Oh, Nurse. Tell Ellen how beautiful Mama was.

NURSE. Rachelle? She was one pretty woman. Even in her casket she looked about twenty-five. Long brown hair and big blue eyes. Rachelle was my little girl. Couldn't have none of my own. She liked big showy hats, purple ribbons, shoes, hats, and you. "Hand me my baby," she'd say. But mostly I remember she was beautiful. Beautiful the day she was born and beautiful the day she died. *(Pause)* Now you...you look like them Trowells, your papa's people, 'cept you 'bout your mama's height and you...you got her hands. That's right. *(Wipes her eyes)*

SOPHIE. Don't cry. I'm sure Mama's in heaven. Read our fortunes.

(NURSE reads Tarot cards.)

NURSE. What shall I look for?

SOPHIE. Oh, romance. For Ellen and me.

NURSE. Oh, my...The lover's card by the devil?

SOPHIE. Is that bad?

NURSE. Ain't always bad. Devil can mean...warm nights and—

ELLEN. What's that?

NURSE. Death card. Now...It don't always mean death.

SOPHIE. Could be the money problems Uncle's having?

NURSE. That ain't the feeling I'm getting here. To me... *(Looks at* **ELLEN***)* Somebody want what ain't right.

*(***NURSE** *exits.)*

ELLEN. I hope you all don't think I married the professor for money.

SOPHIE. Nobody said that.

ELLEN. I'd no dowry, true, but we'd wonderful times...I grew up in Ocean Springs, a town so small that people rushed to their windows when a stranger arrived. The Professor was an icon in New Orleans. He taught me to curtsy and to decorate a man's arm. *(The girls waltz.)*

SOPHIE. Is it hard being married to an older man?

ELLEN. Sometimes. Now we don't discuss anything because we don't—

SOPHIE. Get along?

ELLEN. But we go for drives together, sometimes. "I don't need much affection," he says.

SOPHIE. Even in bed?

ELLEN. Sophie! You want to embarrass me? Last Saturday, he fell asleep when I was kissing him, shut his eyes and began to snore. I shook him, but he wouldn't wake up. Next morning I thought he'd redeem himself, but he said nothing. *(They laugh.)*

SOPHIE. I too am baffled by love.

ELLEN. For the doctor? He's the "prince" of rural Louisiana.

SOPHIE. He discovered medicine on the plantation infirmary.

ELLEN. Worshiping a man is easier than living with one.

SOPHIE. I should stop myself, but it feels so good to think about him. *(Giggles)*

ELLEN. Let's...celebrate your discovery. Drink to friendship and the doctor. *(Footsteps. She calls out to the Watchman.)* Is that you, night watchman? Quiet when you pass my husband's window. But here, play something lively and loud.

SOPHIE. I'd better ask Papa. Too much noise upsets him.

(Exits. Harmonica plays, "In the Good Old Summertime.")

(SOUND: "After The Ball.")

ELLEN. It's so long since I've danced. Spun about a room. But tonight, I shall cry and dance and dance and cry. Then I'll nap in the guest bedroom: pull down the mosquito bars, wrap myself in sky-blue sheets, and gaze at the canopy of cupids, whirling through the stars. Drift to a nocturnal place partly in time, partly in eternity.

(ELLEN dances to a frenzy. SOPHIE returns.)

SOPHIE. Papa says we can't dance.

(MAMERE enters, followed by the NURSE.)

MAMERE. Dance? Did I hear the word dance?

NURSE. She's up.

ELLEN. Let's kick up our heels.

MAMERE. And drink a mint julep.

NURSE. We'd some parties here.

SOPHIE. Shush.

MAMERE. Watching, smelling and—

ELLEN. Sampling bubbling sugar?

SOPHIE. Not so loud.

MAMERE. I stopped the hallway clock—

NURSE. When the guests arrived—

MAMERE. And kept it off—

NURSE. Until they left.

ELLEN. Were there roses?

MAMERE. Everywhere—

SOPHIE. On the mantles?

NURSE. Tables, and stairs—

MAMERE. Thirty bouquets—

SOPHIE. Of long-stemmed—

ELLEN. Red roses?

NURSE. And cake.

MAMERE. We danced out here—

NURSE. Caught a breeze.

SOPHIE. Sang and ate—

ELLEN. Duck?

NURSE. Snipe—

MAMERE. And quail.

SOPHIE. And drank—

ELLEN. Champagne?

NURSE. And dreamed of—

MAMERE. Marriages that'd take us—

ELLEN. To the ends—

SOPHIE. Of the world!

(LIGHTS: The women dance wildly as the lights fade.)

Scene 2

(A week later. There is a table with account books and papers. A smaller table with the doctor's charts. Daytime. **NURSE** *and the* **DOCTOR** *are onstage. She is making a quilt and singing. He drinks.)*

DOCTOR. Who's the quilt for?

NURSE. Special girl. Which colors do you like?

DOCTOR. Yellow...and blue.

NURSE. Blue's the girl's favorite shade, but she likes fiery colors too. I'll put sunshine and sky in here. Which flowers you remember smelling as a child?

DOCTOR. I'm not much on quilts—gardenias.

NURSE. I'll look for that. I've a closet of scraps from my Mama and my Grandma. For years they sewed to keep their sanity, arranging scraps by color: coral, turquoise, plum, and toffee. Feel that beauty. *(He touches the fabric.)* It helps cope with loss to have a real live patchwork quilt.

DOCTOR. I wouldn't know.

NURSE. Quilting is a hopeful way of dealing with life. I try to make sense of things by living each moment I sew. I play with patches and let my mind roam. Smell this? *(Holds up a scrap, which he takes.)* Each color has a scent: intense red, rich amber, water blue, sweet vanilla. Wha'd you smell?

DOCTOR. Not sure.

NURSE. A drop of oak moss! I don't know about you. You come to dinner, but go home by yourself. You end up being connected to everybody and nobody.

DOCTOR. I can't afford a wife.

NURSE. Some women don't need money. They need a promise.

*(*SOPHIE *enters with a vase, followed by* **VICTOR** *with some wildflowers, and* **ELLEN** *with writing paper. The following speeches overlap.)*

SOPHIE. Papa wants us to meet here—

VICTOR. The minute the cutting begins, he starts. Cut down that cane and watch him pontificate—

SOPHIE. He wants to report about the progress he's made.

VICTOR. And what I've failed to do, while I exhaust myself with work crews. Sorry. I'm from a Jesuit education, so I always thought the heart of any great movement was terror. Yesterday, I lost my temper. I threw a book at him and told him to stop bullying me. I was amazed. He backed off.

ELLEN. He was in a foul mood last night.

VICTOR. I can't sleep, remembering his snipes. He feels great afterwards and I feel whipped.

SOPHIE. I'm sure he's doing what's best.

VICTOR. —For himself. He sits in his chair, sets up his suspicions, justifies being mean. I have to hold back or I'll spend the whole day hollering.

SOPHIE. He improved after my meeting with him. He said, "Did you notice I was pleasant?"

ELLEN. He's upset because he may have heart disease.

VICTOR. He's a—hypochondriac. This morning he left me a note that the right side of the house needed painting. As if I don't know. I purposefully avoid walking by that side, so I don't have to see it.

SOPHIE. It'll take months before he accepts he can't live like he used to. I'll check on him. *(Exits.)*

*(*VICTOR *begins arranging flowers.* **ELLEN** *stretches out and polishes her ring against her skirt—looks outside.)*

VICTOR. *(Watches her)* What are you doing?

ELLEN. I'm counting the holes in the clouds. I suppose you think I'm incapable of meditation.

VICTOR. Just lazy. Follow your desires.

ELLEN. I wanted to spend the day writing letters, but I lack the courage.

VICTOR. You could straighten your quarters. Embroider? A woman who can't sew is as slow as a man who can't ride.

ELLEN. I'm going to lie in the shade. Watch the leaves. See how long I can do nothing.

(SOPHIE enters.)

SOPHIE. Papa's still eating.

VICTOR. That's it. I wait for no one over twenty minutes.

(Exits. SOPHIE toys with a flower.)

SOPHIE. I wish you could've seen them when Mama was alive. So full and thick. (*Pause)* Beauty is so seductive to men.

ELLEN. It's easy to seduce men.

SOPHIE. But not the doctor. He undertakes jaunts, jumping into his carriage with his charts, but he doesn't notice me.

ELLEN. I'm sure he likes you.

SOPHIE. I'm not sure. I keep looking back, reliving my memories. Wondering if he has this same excited discontent. I'm afraid to be around him for fear he'll see how lightheaded I am with him. Everyone knows I'm in love with him. The servants, Nurse, Uncle. I can't bear the embarrassment. What should I do? I weigh his pauses for meaning.

ELLEN. I'll question him.

SOPHIE. Oh, would you? It's hard to say, "Won't you marry me?"

ELLEN. I'll get the doctor to the side. I'll tell him not to return if he doesn't love you.

SOPHIE. And if he does—

ELLEN. I'll say when it comes to rings, size doesn't matter.

SOPHIE. Oh, Lord, I'm so delighted—

(Exits)

ELLEN. *(Alone)* What good's this mausoleum to a girl whose blood's raging. Has she ever been courted? He doesn't love her. And I'm wild for him. Suspended in animation, actively captured. She doesn't see our chemistry because she's too compliant. Maybe...I should help her. *(The* **DOCTOR** *enters, carrying charts and maps.)* Shouldn't you be going?

DOCTOR. The only reason I go home's to see my dog. I've a giant Schnauzer whose parents are champions. He was sired in Russia. *(Takes out a chart)*

ELLEN. How do you have time for these charts of the river with so many patients?

DOCTOR. Some nights I'm bone idle, and the Mississippi fills up the evening for me. I update these charts. *(Unrolls a map)* Years ago when the Choctaws roamed, the river front was dense green, thousands of trees...You're not interested.

ELLEN. I am. What are those marks?

DOCTOR. Holes where trees were.

ELLEN. And the x's?

DOCTOR. Houses destroyed but not replaced. Homeless are everywhere. People lock their gates against men who don't have the energy to come up the drive for a crust of bread. I ease the moans of the dying.

ELLEN. How do you face the family?

DOCTOR. When I look into their cold eyes and whitened cheeks, and say, "I'm sorry," they know.

ELLEN. Just out of curiosity, is it over with you and Sophie?

DOCTOR. You don't need circuitous tactics—

ELLEN. So, the answer's "no"?

DOCTOR. You know why I'm here. I don't come for food. Victor's food would worm a dog. Let's go somewhere.

ELLEN. Where will we go?

DOCTOR. Walk on the levee, dine over a crack before it's sacked and closed. Contemplate the beautiful bruised colors of the Mississippi.

ELLEN. Like an aphrodisiac.

DOCTOR. Yes. Feel the wind, smell the fecundity in the air. Erase ourselves in the screaming blackness. *(Pause)* Come here. It's more interesting to embrace when there's a sense of penalty.

ELLEN. Please leave.

DOCTOR. You feel nothing for me? I caught those glances. That scared sadness.

ELLEN. I'm getting my husband.

DOCTOR. While you're talking, he leaves the room—Interrupts when you get enthusiastic. *(Pause)* First time I saw you in that black silk gown, your hair flowing by your face, I thought you might be a siren.

ELLEN. No closer!

DOCTOR. *(He takes her in his arms.)* I want to smell your hair.

ELLEN. Move—

DOCTOR. Like sweet olive trees.

ELLEN. ...no.

DOCTOR. Or a trail of honeysuckle—

ELLEN. Don't . . .

DOCTOR. Falling, half-lost toward—

ELLEN. Stop.

DOCTOR. Lush camellias and beds of wood violets. *(She breaks away. A hard silence.)* I've gone into a terrible decline waiting for you. Replaying your words. Reliving scenes because they haunt me when I'm calming myself before going into surgery.

ELLEN. You...shouldn't—

DOCTOR. Soothed by your particular strange voice . . .

ELLEN. Do that.

DOCTOR. Thinking what it'd be like—

ELLEN. Oh, God...no.

DOCTOR. To have what I want.

(Grabs her and kisses her as **VICTOR** *enters with a bouquet of roses. The following lines overlap.)*

VICTOR. You should ring a bell when it's safe to enter.

ELLEN. We're just good friends—

VICTOR. —Good friends . . .

ELLEN. —It was nothing.

VICTOR. Two and two are four; not three or five.

ELLEN. I'll fix those roses.

VICTOR. Don't touch them with your...white hands of deception. They belong in a...glorious church with frescoes...You're becoming a witch...and that's a...uh, death sentence—The number of witches burned over the centuries is nine million. Shriveled women with pendulous breasts—*(VICTOR faces the* **DOCTOR.***)* And you...you! You don't like women. You do everything but the carnal act. My best friend stabs me in the back.

DOCTOR. I thought you knew—

VICTOR. Sorry. I wasn't paying attention to the obvious.

(As the **DOCTOR** *exits,* **SOPHIE** *enters and whispers to* **ELLEN***.)*

SOPHIE. Did you talk to the doctor? What did he say? Tell me quick. *(ELLEN sighs.)* Your eyes say it all.

(SOPHIE covers her mouth. The **PROFESSOR** *enters with a bowl, sees* **VICTOR** *with the roses standing by* **ELLEN***, and speaks sharply.)*

RANDOLPH. I just tried the bread pudding. I've got to consume the whole thing. *(Sits and eats. The others watch and wait.)*

SOPHIE. Did you have a good nap?

RANDOLPH. So-so.

VICTOR. Only so-so?

RANDOLPH. *(Jovial)* So-so is good for me. You all may hate me, but I...I won't go on a glider and do nothing but idle.

VICTOR. No one wishes you to.

RANDOLPH. Sit in a rocker with parasites for friends, then take my place among the tombs bordered by ironwork. Sophie, get the books. I want to thank Victor for handling my property. The man's worked nineteen years and we agreed he'd make all the little decisions, and I'd make the big ones. And so far I've never had any decisions. All kidding aside, I've serious matters to discuss. As you know, I appreciate how generous you've all been. Victor does the best he can, but Waverly has been a burden. Poor fellow wasn't raised to do much. And when was the last time Mamere had a new gown? When I tell you all the good news, I don't want you to thank me all at once. I've gone to considerable lengths to assess the value of our assets and I've discovered we're millionaires. Millionaires on paper, that is. I, of course, was born a poor boy, so money doesn't mean that much to me. Money can't buy happiness. Yes, I had to work for an education, wear used clothes, save string. I'm a well-known professor but I've had to rely on Victor, Sophie and Mamere for advice on practical family matters. I'm old, sick. I never thought I'd see my sixtieth year. How many good days do I have left? Still, I can't think of myself. I've a young wife and an unmarried daughter to consider. *(Pause)* We can't go on living here. We're not country people. What's the point of having a beautiful wife if you can't be seen with her and take her out? We can't afford to live in New Orleans on the income we get from Waverly. Were we to sell the woods, swamps, or mineral rights, those are one-time transactions and couldn't be repeated. We need a way to guarantee ourselves a fixed income. Now, I've devised a plan that'll please everyone, including Victor, and I'd like to outline it to you.

VICTOR. How long will this take?

RANDOLPH. A few minutes. I need everyone's opinion. The average return on the sugar plantation is about three percent a year. I propose we sell the place, invest the proceeds in managed funds at six percent and set aside a few thousand for a small house in New Orleans.

VICTOR. Wait. I think I'm going deaf. Repeat what you just said.

RANDOLPH. That we invest the proceeds in managed funds and buy a small house—

VICTOR. No. No. You said something before—

RANDOLPH. I propose we sell the place.

VICTOR. That's it. Sell "the place." THE PLACE. Great idea. Fantastic! And where do you propose I live? And Mama? And Sophie?

RANDOLPH. Let's not jump ahead. We don't have to decide all the details—

VICTOR. Wait, I...I'm losing whatever sense I had. I seem to recall, tell me if I'm wrong, that "this place" belongs to Sophie. My sister and I put it in trust as a dowry for her. Sophie is to take charge of the property when she marries or when you die.

RANDOLPH. Sophie's whom I'm thinking about.

SOPHIE. Don't bring me into this. I want what is good for you all.

RANDOLPH. Of course this place is for Sophie. Who said anything to the contrary? I wouldn't sell without her permission. What I'm proposing is for her benefit.

VICTOR. Preposterous. I don't believe what I'm hearing. I must be asleep or in some nightmare.

MAMERE. Victor, don't raise your voice at Randolph. He knows best.

VICTOR. I need a drink. Some bourbon. God. Give me some sherry, straight alcohol. Anything. Go on, say whatever you want. Say it. Say it. Go.

RANDOLPH. I don't understand what gets into you. Why are you so upset? I know my proposal's not ideal, but it is a way out. If you all think I'm being extreme, okay, I won't insist.

VICTOR. I maintain what I can, but the lack of money makes my job impossible.

RANDOLPH. I'm not blaming you, but vegetation's gone wild, brickwork's in a shambles—

VICTOR. You think I don't see? Still, I made sure you didn't go a day without a drive in your red fringed carriage.

RANDOLPH. True...but—*(Looks at* **ELLEN***)* What's a young woman to do here, walk slowly, parasol in hand, feeding the ducks? Avoid the sun. Try not to use light too much inside as it intensifies heat. Let her life simmer for a long time so it won't spoil. *(Looks at* **SOPHIE***)* And poor Sophie, she's orphaned in a way. What husband will she find? A farm hand? Males under thirty-five are the real ghosts on Louisiana's plantations. I see now. We must adjust to the new situation and perhaps sell Waverly.

MAMERE. I don't understand.

RANDOLPH. If Victor's at the auction, he can bid and keep it in the family.

SOPHIE. He's still paying off your excesses: thirteen check shirts, twenty-seven silk handkerchiefs, thirty-nine broadcloth vests—don't tease him now.

RANDOLPH. I'm not. I feel bad. Waverly's got a manager who's desperate and worries all the time. In the city, from sale revenue, he could enjoy peace of mind. We'll tell the Sheriff we want the best price—

MAMERE. You don't mean to . . .

RANDOLPH. From the best buyer—

NURSE. To sell this estate . . .

RANDOLPH. And we're shopping around. It shouldn't be difficult—

SOPHIE. After Uncle sacrificed his life, his...youth.

RANDOLPH. I don't think he works hard. He says he inspects the fields. Most times he's off exploring the countryside, reading journals, and gossiping with the help. I don't mind. He should enjoy himself. Meanwhile, the invoices rise. *(Opens book)* We can't pay for these repairs. The roof leaks; the ceilings are cracked; and all the floors giving in places. *(Pause)* Look at the debit columns. How can we sustain a sugar business that at best breaks even? A business that depends on good weather in a state where weather's precarious.

SOPHIE. Our ancestors did it.

RANDOLPH. On the backs of slaves. *(Pause)* We can't even meet the taxes and insurance. *(To* **SOPHIE***)* I'm looking out for your concerns. Let's leave before we have to be carried out.

VICTOR. Enough! What do you know about hard work? Lying about like a lizard in the sun.

RANDOLPH. Don't take out your—

VICTOR. All lizards used to be reptiles—

RANDOLPH. Don't punish my wife. Nothing's decided yet . . .

VICTOR. I've worn myself out. Up at dawn noting every task is done—Under rigid control with stringent economy.

RANDOLPH. It's good you did.

VICTOR. We've the mortgage paid off—

RANDOLPH. We appreciate it—

VICTOR. Sophie has a dowry.

RANDOLPH. I know, but you're half a saint. You've the promise to get there, but you're still carrying the cross.

VICTOR. I don't believe what I'm hearing. I denounce all rights to my inheritance, except for the rear cottage—I don't know why I did this, but Sister said, "I'd like Sophie to have Waverly. Normally an estate passes to a son, but Sophie's your heir, and she's—"

SOPHIE. Plain. Yes.

VICTOR. Sister didn't say plain. She said you were—

SOPHIE. Ugly.

VICTOR. Quiet. I slave to bring Waverly into solvency.

SOPHIE. Even sold bricks from Mama's gardens.

VICTOR. The place finally brings in revenue. Granted, it's a pittance, but you can't sell Waverly—

SOPHIE. Without consulting Uncle.

RANDOLPH. I can. I hear him and I don't agree with him.

SOPHIE. Mamere, we can't let Waverly go.

NURSE. When you think of what this house has witnessed.

RANDOLPH. It's not my fault we don't have enough money.

VICTOR. I won't let you do this.

RANDOLPH. I'd like to save this plantation. But I'm your brother-in-law. I'm not God. Waverly's sinking, moron. "They ain't going to be nothing for nobody," we don't bail out.

VICTOR. You're so brutal.

RANDOLPH. Why can't you get it...get it through your thick skull. Waverly's going down the drain. Grab your life vest. In one swoop we're going under.

*(*RANDOLPH *tries to stand.* VICTOR *pushes him down. They fight.)*

VICTOR. No, we're not.

RANDOLPH. It's hard to believe you're a grown man in your forties. Since I arrived, you've tortured me. You're envious. I was a successful professor for thirty years, but that's over. I apologize. After twenty-nine days at Waverly, I've had enough. I won't turn into a blind man. Live here in a big bed and draw the shutters. I'm going to sell Waverly, and you can either go screaming and crying, or you can walk out with dignity like sensible adults.

VICTOR. *(To* **RANDOLPH***)* You won't get away with this.

SOPHIE. We're losing Waverly!

MAMERE. Not Waverly. Mama hid her silver in a compartment on the wall. And my brothers carved initials in the floor.

VICTOR. Sister wouldn't have stood for this. Who would have thought Randolph would have finagled her will.

MAMERE. Everyone said he was so brilliant, he threw off a light.

51

VICTOR. And now...After climbing the university ladder, he's created a trumped-up trusteeship to justify theft.

MAMERE. Poor Victor can't get to the first rung of the ladder.

VICTOR. Oh God...What should I do, Mama?

MAMERE. I don't think you'll learn until right before you die.

VICTOR. We can't let him sell Waverly.

MAMERE. No, it's a millennium house with open doors, high ceilings and cross-ventilation. It'll take one thousand years to forget all that.

RANDOLPH. Mrs. Mallory.

VICTOR. Don't go near her.

RANDOLPH. You look so young.

VICTOR. Talk to her! Touch her!

MAMERE. *(Pats* **RANDOLPH***'s hand)* I suppose you can't stay at Waverly and amount to anything?

RANDOLPH. No. We'll ease into the new glitz with gleaming luggage and for you a Canadian fox fur coat.

MAMERE. Well...if the professor says go, let's go. I just realized how capable he is. I'm so used to Victor—

VICTOR. How can you say that, Mama?

MAMERE. I was being facetious.

VICTOR. Go ahead. Turn my life into a joke! *(To* **RANDOLPH***)* You're a snake. Satan!

(Exits)

RANDOLPH. I don't need your permission to sell what's mine.

SOPHIE. Uncle's irreplaceable.

RANDOLPH. The cemeteries are full of irreplaceable people.

ELLEN. Don't leave him so upset.

SOPHIE. Make up, Papa!

RANDOLPH. To keep Waverly, you need a wizard with a pot of gold....You can't reason with a jackass. *(A shot is heard behind the scenes. A shriek from* **ELLEN. NURSE** *runs out, followed by* **SOPHIE.***)* Somebody go get...get him. He's lost his mind.

*(*VICTOR *staggers in.* **ELLEN** *and* **VICTOR** *struggle in the doorway.)*

ELLEN. Give me the pistol...

MAMERE. Lord!

VICTOR. Where is he?

SOPHIE. Stop!

ELLEN. Give...

NURSE. It's loaded.

VICTOR....Thank...God.

ELLEN. I'm taking it.

VICTOR. Move.

MAMERE. Wait...I...

NURSE. Careful!

SOPHIE. Watch out!

VICTOR. Where...is he?

MAMERE. Don't shoot.

VICTOR. I'm going to...kill him. Ahhh! *(They struggle.* **VICTOR** *frees himself from* **ELLEN**. *Runs about looking for* **RANDOLPH**.*)* I'll find the...the...coward!

ELLEN. Oh God, no...

VICTOR. And kill him.

SOPHIE AND **MAMERE.** Don't! No!

ELLEN. Duck!

VICTOR. Lucifer!

(VICTOR fires at **RANDOLPH**. *Bang. A pause.)*

RANDOLPH. Vicious bastard. You think you can come in here—

VICTOR. I missed him.

RANDOLPH. And take my life.

VICTOR. *(Furious,* **VICTOR** *fires again and misses.)* Damn. Hell. Can't...even shoot...A lousy gun.

*(***RANDOLPH** *is overwhelmed.* **ELLEN** *leans against a wall and almost faints.)*

ELLEN. Get me out of here.

RANDOLPH. What've I done?

VICTOR. After how I treated him... *(***VICTOR** *puts gun to his own head.)*

*(***SOPHIE** *screams)*

SOUND: "Dixie Land."

VICTOR. No more bullets.

*(***ELLEN** *laughs)*

Scene 3

(Later. **NURSE** *sings.* **DOCTOR** *drinks. Then he searches his medical bag for something.* **NURSE** *rises.)*

DOCTOR. Don't leave.

NURSE. I got to help them pack. It's a sad day. That's all I got to say. Can't you do nothing to set things right? Give the poor girl some hope.

DOCTOR. Who? What?

NURSE. Sophie needs to get married. I send her in here, and you do it.

(Exits quickly. Footsteps. **VICTOR** *enters and tosses the gun to the* **DOCTOR.***)*

DOCTOR. Where've you been?

VICTOR. I'm not sure. I don't know whether I was drunk or not but I woke up with this headache, looked up at the ceiling, and thought, "Am I in hell?"

DOCTOR. Give me what you stole from me.

VICTOR. *(Ignores him)* You think I'm mad? A person torments you hourly, you take one shot at him, and they say you're crazy. And you...

DOCTOR. When you let men bully you—They'll persist.

VICTOR. I wore patched sleeves—

DOCTOR. Darned socks.

VICTOR. Oh, give me something. I'm disgusted.

DOCTOR. Half of humanity is disgusted, but you're acting like an idiot. Maybe three hundred years from now, people will know how to be happy. They'll look back at us and laugh: working unsuccessfully—trying to speak right, to find answers, to cure things. They'll be smarter and wiser and they'll resurrect hope. *(Pause)* Don't kill yourself with that morphia you stole from me.

VICTOR. You can do my post mortem.

DOCTOR. That's nice. I get to identify the fact my morphia killed you? If you need drugs, let me introduce you to my best friend Johnny Walker—Because you can stop drinking—

VICTOR. I can't face Randolph.

DOCTOR. You'll have to.

VICTOR. Why can't I sleep and never wake up! I cheapened myself for lust. *(To **DOCTOR**)* You—BETRAYED ME—my best friend. You knew I loved Ellen. A FRIENDSHIP DIED HERE. You were more intelligent, more sensitive than the rest. BETRAYING ME FOR THAT... THAT... nothing's left. *(Pause)* I'm forty-two. I'll live another twenty or thirty years. How? If only I'd wake up in a different place, in a younger, more virile-looking body. I'm wearing out. You don't see it. It's the old enthusiasm that's gone. Tell me how can I start a new life. They must teach you what to tell patients. That's what I need to know.

DOCTOR. *(Extends gun)* Here, kill yourself. Shoot. Be done with it.

*(**SOPHIE** enters.)*

SOPHIE. Oh no. I'll put that pistol somewhere safe.

DOCTOR. First help me get the morphia your uncle stole from me.

SOPHIE. *(To **VICTOR**)* You stole morphia?

VICTOR. I can't take living.

SOPHIE. How come women can take it? Men can't...I am just as unhappy as you are.

VICTOR. Oh, here. *(Shoves her the bottle)* But you better pull things together—

SOPHIE. What should I do? What?

VICTOR. Figure it out. You're so capable.

SOPHIE. All right...I will. *(Hands **DOCTOR** the bottle)*

*(**ELLEN** enters, looks at the doctor, **SOPHIE**, **VICTOR**.)*

ELLEN. We're leaving.

DOCTOR. I can go now.

ELLEN. How are you feeling?

VICTOR. Don't patronize me.

ELLEN. The professor wants to speak to you.

DOCTOR. That's good.

VICTOR. I can't handle more degradation.

ELLEN. Forgive him for his flaws.

DOCTOR. You could do that...don't you think?

ELLEN. And the good things he taught—

SOPHIE. Will live in you.

VICTOR....I'm sorry...demanding people offend me—All right. One final sermon.

(SOPHIE and VICTOR exit. The DOCTOR looks at ELLEN.)

DOCTOR. Can't you sit?

ELLEN. It'd be foolish.

DOCTOR. Foolish me. Shut your eyes.

ELLEN. I'm so tired...The professor wants everything—

DOCTOR. Rest. Try feeling once and for all satiated—

ELLEN. *(The DOCTOR takes her hand.)* What are you doing? Oh no...

DOCTOR. Checking your pulse. That's all.

ELLEN....well, be quick.

DOCTOR. Your breathing's rushed. Excuse the cold hands—

ELLEN. Don't. —Will you try to believe that I am a good person?

DOCTOR. You don't love anyone. You are a hedonist. Why not follow your feelings?

ELLEN. Stop!

DOCTOR. I'm amenable to just looking.

ELLEN. No. I...I can't meet your needs...

DOCTOR. Good.

ELLEN. I'm sorry if I've given you the—

DOCTOR. Let's celebrate uncertainty.

ELLEN. Impression that I wanted an—

DOCTOR. Let's run off somewhere! Oh, Ellen. I'm giving you a chance for a face near you, by you, a face that loves you.

*(*DOCTOR *takes her in his arms.)*

ELLEN.....I think...I can't deal with . . .

DOCTOR. My feelings for you! And what we could do about them! Can't you see something's missing from your life? You're bound to give in to a brush with passion. Do it where there's nature to hide you. A man that loves you. Even this far. I feel you. I sense the blood in your veins. I see your body living in me, shining through me. Run away with me—

ELLEN. I won't. I . . .

DOCTOR. And you'll no longer weep for your life. *(*DOCTOR *grabs* ELLEN*.)*

ELLEN. I...I can't go. Not now. I come from a different world.

DOCTOR. You could change.

ELLEN. I feel too old...If a woman is going to stray, it'll be in her early twenties. By her late twenties, she's resigned to how miserable life is.

DOCTOR. Yes, you should go away. There is something strange about you. You and your husband just showed up here one day. We were all busy working, doing things. You infected us like yellow fever!...I haven't done a thing for over a month, and there are a lot of sick people out there. So what do I do now? Abandon my practice? I see you every day and suddenly I won't see you again. I'll breathe, eat, drink and sleep but there will be no life!

ELLEN....Forgive me. *(She rushes to him and kisses him passionately)*

(Sound of footsteps. They break apart. Enter **RANDOLPH**, **VICTOR** *followed by* **MAMERE**, **NURSE**, *and* **SOPHIE**.*)*

RANDOLPH. I just want to tell you, Victor, you're an incredibly good man. Forget the past.

VICTOR. . . . How can I?

RANDOLPH. Don't talk about it. Forgiveness is a superior act to vengeance.

VICTOR. You're right but I'm not open to change; change unnerves me.

RANDOLPH. Imitate me. I like to learn and to teach, and I flatter myself that I'm good at both.

VICTOR. Still, you're owed an apology. For what I did out here—

RANDOLPH. Not another word. *(Looks up)* What a clear sky.

VICTOR. I didn't notice. I've been through so much, I anticipate disappointment...even bad weather. I carry an umbrella even though it hasn't rained for days.

RANDOLPH. I hate to leave...but I've to get Ellen in the carriage before dark. *(She nods.)* I want to drive by the chapel where we married and check on the family tomb. That sepulcher was inspired by Michelangelo's Pièta. And the tombs of the Medici princes. *(To* **ELLEN***)* Give me your hand, sweetheart.

SOPHIE. Say a prayer for me by Mama's grave—

RANDOLPH. I'll describe the flora and fauna that inspired Audubon—

MAMERE. Isn't the professor a genius? He's the ambassador of this family. If only Victor could have learned something from him.

RANDOLPH. Ah, it's Victor we should thank, Mamere. Soon as I get to the city, I'm going to send you the right fluff. A little fur for your coat.

MAMERE. Such extravagance!

(SOUND: Carriage bells ring.)

(Carriage arrives for **PROFESSOR.***)*

RANDOLPH. You must excuse me.

SOPHIE. Oh, Papa. I don't want you to leave.

MAMERE. You sure I can't go with you? *(He nods no.)* Well, mail me the first draft of your next article so I can study it.

NURSE. She'll look every day. Don't forget to write.

RANDOLPH. I'll get Ellen to send a long letter. *(Chuckles)* She's nothing better to do. I'm being facetious. *(He and* **VICTOR** *embrace.)* Life's short, and there's no time to thank people enough.

VICTOR. I'll pay you the same as before.

RANDOLPH. Don't trouble too much. You've worked for twenty years—

VICTOR. Everything shall be as it was. Maybe I can do better.

RANDOLPH. For now...Ellen and I'll live like little love mice. One room's enough for us honeymooners. *(Looks at the* **DOCTOR.***)* I'd a catharsis last night. Talked to the wee hours with my wife. We'll be cozy in closer quarters. *(He puts an arm around her and she breaks free to hug* **SOPHIE.***)*

ELLEN. I'll miss you.

SOPHIE. Write to us. When you settle down.

RANDOLPH. Goodbye, everybody.

VICTOR. *(Kisses* **ELLEN***)* We'll probably never meet again.

RANDOLPH. I'll remember you all . . .

ELLEN. Maybe not.

VICTOR. Pardon me for anything I've done.

ELLEN. Of course.

RANDOLPH. We're off. I'll remember you all. So much emotion and appreciation. I'm surprised. Delighted. I'm taking a lifetime sabbatical with my bride. Ellen, put your arm through mine. Smile and wave goodbye.

*(*RANDOLPH *and* ELLEN *exit, followed by* NURSE, *and* MAMERE. DOCTOR *speaks to* SOPHIE.*)*

DOCTOR. So long. Please bring my carriage around?

*(*SOPHIE *goes out. The* DOCTOR *and* VICTOR *remain. The* DOCTOR *drinks with no food. He is becoming an alcoholic.* VICTOR *loses himself in his ledgers. Each man murmurs to himself but the words overlap.)*

DOCTOR. We should wave them off.

VICTOR. I was never one for long goodbyes.

DOCTOR. They're getting in the carriage.

(SOUND: Sound of carriage bells.)

VICTOR. Sophie hasn't balanced the books.

DOCTOR. Ellen takes with her some kind of unspeakable music.

VICTOR. When you stop subtracting figures, you think you've more money than you've got.

DOCTOR. She didn't proceed with explanations. She appreciated mystery.

VICTOR. Invoices are lined up against me.

DOCTOR. Her life and mine were intertwined. We should've been friends forever.

VICTOR. I've got to hurry to see which bills can wait.

(SOUND: Carriage.)

DOCTOR. She came when the leaves were full on the trees and went when they were gone. How quiet it is. There's no rain or wind. Just the sound of a lone squirrel. Terribly silent and safe here. The dim light full of meditative sadness. I've this sense that life is leaving me. Mmm. They're gone.

*(Enter **SOPHIE**.)*

SOPHIE. They're gone. Strange chill in the air rolling in from some polar region. Glad I packed blankets. I waved them down the drive like Mama used to do. Stood and waved till there was no more sound, but the flapping of a heron in an oak tree.

(SOUND: Carriage arrives.)

(Holds up a spray of lavender)

SOPHIE. The last of the lavender. It doesn't like our climate. It stayed with us longer than we thought it would—

VICTOR. *(Mumbles to himself)* Delivered to...Mr. Carrerre.

(SOUND: Sound of bells and carriage wheels.)

DOCTOR. My carriage is here. Nothing to do but say goodbye. *(Picks up his bag.)*

SOPHIE. Must you leave?

VICTOR. Sophie!

DOCTOR. Moving's something everybody does.

VICTOR. *(Stamps a letter)* Account delivered. Two dollars and twenty three cents.

DOCTOR. I've this mare with a bad leg. I need to get her home.

SOPHIE. When will you be back?

VICTOR. Sophie, he doesn't know.

DOCTOR. Write if you need me. I'll come, of course.

SOPHIE. Can't you leave tomorrow?

*(DOCTOR starts to leave. **SOPHIE** gets some crackers.)*

DOCTOR. I want to use up all my energy. I don't want any of it to go untried.

SOPHIE. Have some nourishment at least.

DOCTOR. No, thanks.

SOPHIE. A drink?

DOCTOR. *(The* **DOCTOR** *drinks bourbon. Blots his mouth with a handkerchief, puts it down.)* No need to walk me out.

SOPHIE. I want to.

(SOUND: Carriage leaving.)

DOCTOR. No.

*(***MAMERE** *and* **NURSE** *enter,* **MAMERE** *with an article and* **NURSE** *with a quilt.)*

MAMERE. Someone's leaving? Oh, the doctor. I thought he was courting Sophie.

NURSE. Shush now.

MAMERE. I told you it was too soon to work on that trousseau.

NURSE. Mind your own business.

MAMERE. Everybody knows the ring should come before the quilt!

VICTOR. *(Nods and continues writing.)* March the third. Twenty dollars. Friday the fifteenth, twenty dollars again.

(Pause. The sound of bells. **SOPHIE** *enters, puts a candle on the table. Picks up his handkerchief.)*

SOPHIE. The doctor is gone. He left his handkerchief. I've a collection of handkerchiefs. I'll keep this for him.

MAMERE. Did you get a promise? *(***SOPHIE** *nods her head, no.)* Tell him you don't need a big ring.

NURSE. Quiet.

*(***SOPHIE*** lights a candle)*

VICTOR. The house seems empty, as if the walls were laughing.

*(***SOPHIE*** sits at the table with **VICTOR** and writes. **VICTOR** counts. **MAMERE** reads to herself. **NURSE** hums "Amazing Grace.")*

SOPHIE. It's been so long since I sat at this table.

VICTOR. It'll take a week to get it all straight.

MAMERE. I helped Rachelle pick out her linens when she married.

VICTOR. Thirty, thirty-five.

MAMERE. The professor liked my silver pattern.

(The night watchman begins playing "Let Me Call You Sweetheart." **VICTOR** *looks up.)*

SOPHIE. Your books look neat.

VICTOR. It's hard to believe I won't run out of money.

SOPHIE. We must be stronghearted.

VICTOR. *Richard Coeur de Lion.*

SOPHIE. Pray.

VICTOR. For good luck in bad times. Sounds contradictory.

SOPHIE. All prayer is heard. It might not come when we want it, but it's coming.

VICTOR. For most people Waverly is just a name.

SOPHIE. How can you despair when we're surrounded by beauty? Every oak tree is overloaded with an abundance of leaves, so many that they fall.

*(***NURSE** *hums.)*

VICTOR. Twenty three dollars and forty cents. Five dollars... Everything is gone, *mon amie.*

SOPHIE. No, it's not. We can't control whether or not we're successful, but we can control how hard we work. If we keep working, we'll be rewarded. One day we'll wake into the land of angels and dreams and see God in all his brightness. Do you hear? It has just started to rain. The sky is also crying for us.

(SOUND: Ending Music)

THE END

Also by
Rosary Hartel O'Neill...

The Awakening of Kate Chopin

Black Jack: The Thief of Possession

Degas in New Orleans

John Singer Sargent and Madame X

Marilyn/God

Property

Solitaire

Turtle Soup

Uncle Victor

White Suits in Summer

The Wings of Madness

Wishing Aces

OTHER TITLES AVAILABLE FROM SAMUEL FRENCH

PROPERTY

Rosary Hartel O'Neill

Full Length, Southern Comedy / 2m, 3f / Unit set

Property is a contemporary romantic comedy set in a Garden District mansion in New Orleans. Rooster Dubonnet, a young artist suffering from a terminal disease, is dazzled by love. Raised by an imperious society-driven mother, he has fallen in love with a New-Age nurse. Set during Mardi Gras–when a whole tradition of fun, revelry, and prestige seizes the city– Rooster is caught between his dedication to his family's past (and "property") and his own very different future.

OTHER TITLES AVAILABLE FROM SAMUEL FRENCH

THE AWAKENING OF KATE CHOPIN

Rosary Hartel O'Neill

Full Length, Historical Drama / 2m, 2f

Kate Chopin, author of *The Awakening*, struggles to hold onto her marriage and her six small children as she launches her career as a novelist in 1884. Frustrating her attempts are: her wealthy next door neighbor, wanting to prove his masculinity; her jealous husband, stricken with malaria; the little sex-pot seamstress next door, the town gossip; and the bankrupt cotton business, which consumes all of her time. This crazy cacophony of personalities ends up compelling Kate toward her goal of becoming a famous author.

OTHER TITLES AVAILABLE FROM SAMUEL FRENCH

DEGAS IN NEW ORLEANS

Rosary Hartel O'Neill

Full Length, Drama / 3m, 6f / One integrated int/ext set.

A historical drama that explores Edgar Degas' scandalous visit to New Orleans in 1872. Edgar Degas, the French Impressionist painter, is torn between helping his relatives in America and pursuing a career as a painter. Fame and family obligations come to a head when he discovers he is still in love with his sister-in-law, who is now pregnant and blind. As Edgar struggles with his own ethical conundrum, he discovers that his aggressively charming brother has gone through all the family money in an attempt to save his uncle's sugar business.

OTHER TITLES AVAILABLE FROM SAMUEL FRENCH

WHITE SUITS IN SUMMER

Rosary Hartel O'Neill

Full Length, Comedy / 2m, 2f / Unit Set

This contemporary Southern romance set in the topsy-turvy world of art. Celebrity artist Susann is determined to reclaim her lost love, Blaise, now married to a sedate New Orleans socialite. Convinced that she cannot live without him, Susann arranges an exhibition of her works to be held in his new house. Susann's readiness to sacrifice her career, his new wife, and her Mama's boy manager leave Blaise both angry and aroused. Theatrical excitement abounds in this comedy of love vs. duty.

OTHER TITLES AVAILABLE FROM SAMUEL FRENCH

SOLITAIRE

Rosary Hartel O'Neill

Full Length, Southern Comedy / 3m, 2f / Interior

The Mississippi Gulf Coast estate of Irene Dubbonet is an unforgetable place to visit, but who would want to live there? All of her relatives, who hope to inherit it! This is a play about manipulation and what happens to family members' dreams when the odds are stacked against them. A cloud of doom hangs over Serenity Manor, until at last, virtue triumphs. Irene's son, the artist, Rooster, deeply anxious to prove himself, connives a scheme to help his "down and out" brother-in-law seize the estate. Funny situations sparked by witty lines bring the audience into an intriguing overview of topsy-turvy privileged life today.